Lullabies

Kate Toms

Castle Street PRESS

Twinkle, twinkle, little star

Twinkle, twinkle, little star,
how I wonder what you are.
Up above the world so high,
like a diamond in the sky.
Twinkle, twinkle, little star,
how I wonder what you are.

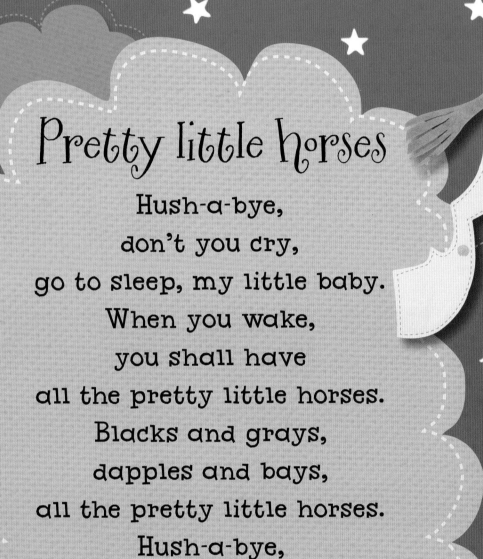

Pretty little horses

Hush-a-bye,
don't you cry,
go to sleep, my little baby.
When you wake,
you shall have
all the pretty little horses.
Blacks and grays,
dapples and bays,
all the pretty little horses.
Hush-a-bye,
don't you cry,
go to sleep, my little baby.
When you wake,
you shall have
all the pretty little horses.

Rock-a-bye, Baby

Rock-a-bye, Baby,
on the treetop.
When the wind blows,
the cradle will rock.
When the bough breaks,
the cradle will fall,
and down will come Baby,
cradle and all.

Hush, little baby

Hush, little baby, don't say a word,
Papa's going to buy you a mockingbird.
And if that mockingbird don't sing,
Papa's going to buy you a diamond ring.
And if that diamond ring turns brass,
Papa's going to buy you a looking glass.

song restorer

very expensive diamond ring

And if that looking glass gets broke,
Papa's going to buy you a billy goat.
And if that billy goat won't pull,
Papa's going to buy you a cart and bull.
And if that cart the bull won't pull,
you'll still be the sweetest child of all.

Lavender's blue

Lavender's blue, dilly, dilly,
lavender's green.
When you are king, dilly, dilly,
I shall be queen.
Who told you so, dilly, dilly,
who told you so?
'Twas my own heart, dilly, dilly,
that told me so.

Wee Willie Winkie

Wee Willie Winkie
runs through the town,
upstairs and downstairs
in his nightgown.
Tapping at the window,
crying through the lock:
Are all the children in their beds?
It's past eight o'clock!

Little Boy Blue

Little Boy Blue,
come blow your horn.
The sheep's in the meadow,
the cow's in the barn,
but where is the boy
who looks after the sheep?
He's under the haystack,
fast asleep!

Baa!

Baa!

Baa!

Bye, Baby Bunting

Bye, Baby Bunting,
Daddy's gone a-hunting,
Mommy's gone a-milking
and Brother's gone
to fetch something
to wrap Baby Bunting in.

I see the moon

I see the moon
and the moon sees me.
God bless the moon
and God bless me.

Sleep, Baby, sleep

Sleep, Baby, sleep,
long and safe and deep.
The wind will blow
the dreamland tree
and from it shake
sweet dreams for thee.
Sleep, Baby, sleep,
our cottage vale is deep.
The little lamb
is on the green,
with snowy fleece
so soft and clean.
Sleep, Baby, sleep.

Come to the window

Come to the window, my baby, with me,
and look at the stars that shine on the sea.
There are bright, little stars that play bo-peep
with two little fish far down in the deep.
And two little frogs cry, neap, neap, neap!
I see a dear baby that should be asleep!